E
MCCOURT

McCourt, Lisa.

Chicken soup for
little souls. Della
Splatnuk birthday
girl.

3254707748099

$14.95

DATE			

CHICKEN SOUP for LITTLE SOULS

Della Splatnuk, Birthday Girl

Story Adaptation by
Lisa McCourt

Illustrated by
Pat Grant Porter

HCI
Health Communications, Inc.
Deerfield Beach, Florida

www.hci-online.com
www.chickensoup.com

Library of Congress Cataloging-in-Publication Data

McCourt, Lisa.
    Chicken soup for little souls. Della Splatnuk birthday girl / story adaptation by Lisa McCourt ;
illustrated by Pat Grant Porter.
        p.   cm.
    "Based on the . . . best-selling series Chicken soup for the soul by Jack Canfield and Mark
Victor Hansen."
    Summary: At first reluctant to attend Della's birthday party because all the kids think that she
was wierd, Carrie finds herself the only guest and decides to make it Della's best birthday ever.
    ISBN 1-55874-600-5 (hard)
    [1. Birthdays—Fiction. 2. Parties—Fiction. 3. Popularity—Fiction. 4. Friendship—Fiction.]
I. Porter, Pat Grant, ill. II. Canfield, Jack, 1944– Chicken soup for the soul. III. Hansen, Mark
Victor. IV. Title. V. Title: Della Splatnuk birthday girl.
PZ7.M47841445Ce   1999
[E]—dc21
                                                                                            98-49908
                                                                                               CIP
                                                                                                AC

©1999 Health Communications, Inc.
ISBN 1-55874-600-5

Story adapted from "Make a Wish" by LeAnne Reaves, *A 3rd Serving of Chicken Soup for the
Soul,* edited by Jack Canfield and Mark Victor Hansen.

Story adaptation ©1999 Lisa McCourt
Illustrations ©1999 Pat Grant Porter

Cover design by Cheryl Nathan

Produced by Boingo Books, Inc.

Publisher: Health Communications, Inc.
             3201 S.W. 15th Street
             Deerfield Beach, FL 33442-8190

Printed in Mexico

For Tucker
—L.M.

For Mara Rose,
Grant and Spenser
—P.G.P.

To Christopher, who has always been
there for any kid who needed a friend
—J.C.

To the genius within each and every one of us
—M.V.H.

To all the birthday girls in my life,
and Melinda and Hayley
—P.V.

I liked parties, but this time I didn't want to go. "It's Della Splatnuk," I said. "She's weird, and Niki and Liz aren't going either. She invited the whole class, all twenty-eight of us."

Mom read the messy invitation again quietly. Della had made all twenty-eight invitations herself, with construction paper and crayons.

"What makes her weird?" Mom asked.

"Everyone just knows she is," I explained. "She has funny hair and she hardly ever talks. Her mother is a fashion designer and she tries out her new styles on Della. Really weird styles. She's just not like the rest of us."

Mom looked sad. Then she said it. "I don't know about anyone else, Carrie, but you're going. I'll pick up a present tomorrow." She gave me a quick hug and went back to her laundry.

I couldn't believe it! She didn't make me go to my cousin's party when I was afraid I wouldn't know anyone and all the kids would be older than me. It wasn't fair.

Saturday afternoon Mom made me wrap the gift she'd bought for me to give Della—an origami kit with special shiny papers. I had gotten the same kit at my birthday party. It was my favorite present.

Then Mom made me put on my newest outfit and
she drove me across town to Della's.

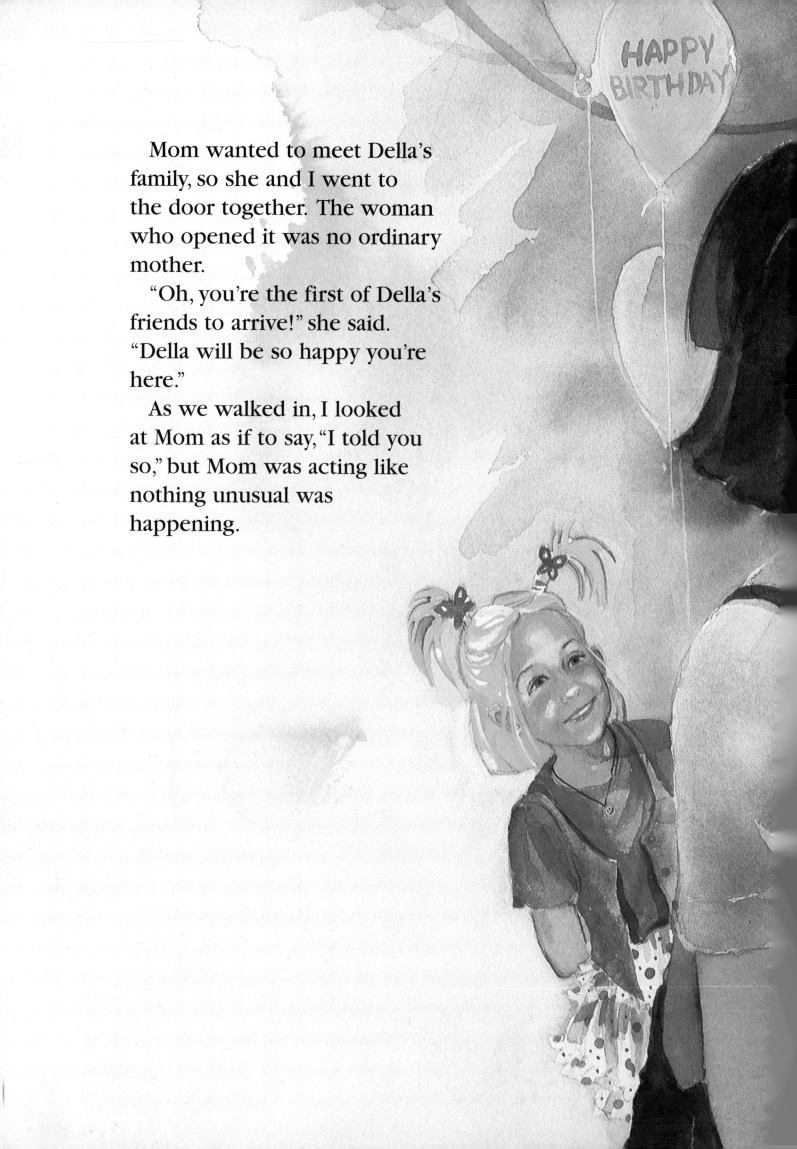

Mom wanted to meet Della's family, so she and I went to the door together. The woman who opened it was no ordinary mother.

"Oh, you're the first of Della's friends to arrive!" she said. "Della will be so happy you're here."

As we walked in, I looked at Mom as if to say, "I told you so," but Mom was acting like nothing unusual was happening.

The house was even stranger than
Della's mother.

At least the table showed signs of a
normal birthday party. In the center was a
huge cake with eight purple candles and
some lumpy rosebuds. "Happy Birthday,
Della" was written in crooked letters across
the top.

Twenty-eight little paper cups filled with candy were spaced evenly around the cake. Each one had a name written on it. *This won't be too bad*, I thought, *once everyone gets here.*

Our two mothers disappeared into the kitchen and I was left face-to-face with Della Splatnuk, the weirdest girl in my school. "So, who else is coming?" I asked.

"I don't know," was all Della said.

I sat down near the door so I could blend in with the kids in
our class as soon as they started showing up. We heard our
mothers laughing in the kitchen. We heard the clock on the wall
tick, tick, ticking. We looked at everything in the room except
each other.

After sitting like that for almost five minutes, the terrible
thought hit me: *No one else was coming.* I just knew it. How
could Mom have made me do this? I was the only one in our
whole class who came!

I was feeling sorry for myself when I heard a sniffle. I looked
across the room to see Della trying hard not to cry, but crying
just the same. Did she really think everyone would come?
Didn't she know what the kids said about her? Maybe she didn't
know. Maybe she hoped her birthday party would be just like
anyone else's. Maybe, just maybe . . . it should have been.

The more I thought about the way my class treated Della, the more I wondered why it had to be that way. Sure, she was quiet and she dressed funny, but what was she really like? Did anyone in my class know? Maybe I could find out.

"Um . . . Della," I asked, "what's your favorite color?"

Della looked up, startled by my question. "Purple," she said.

"That's mine, too," I told her. "Do you like French fries?"

"They're my favorite," she said, wiping the tears from her face.

"Me, too," I said. "Um . . . do you have any pets?"

"No," she said, "but I've always wanted a horse."

I'd always wanted a horse, too.

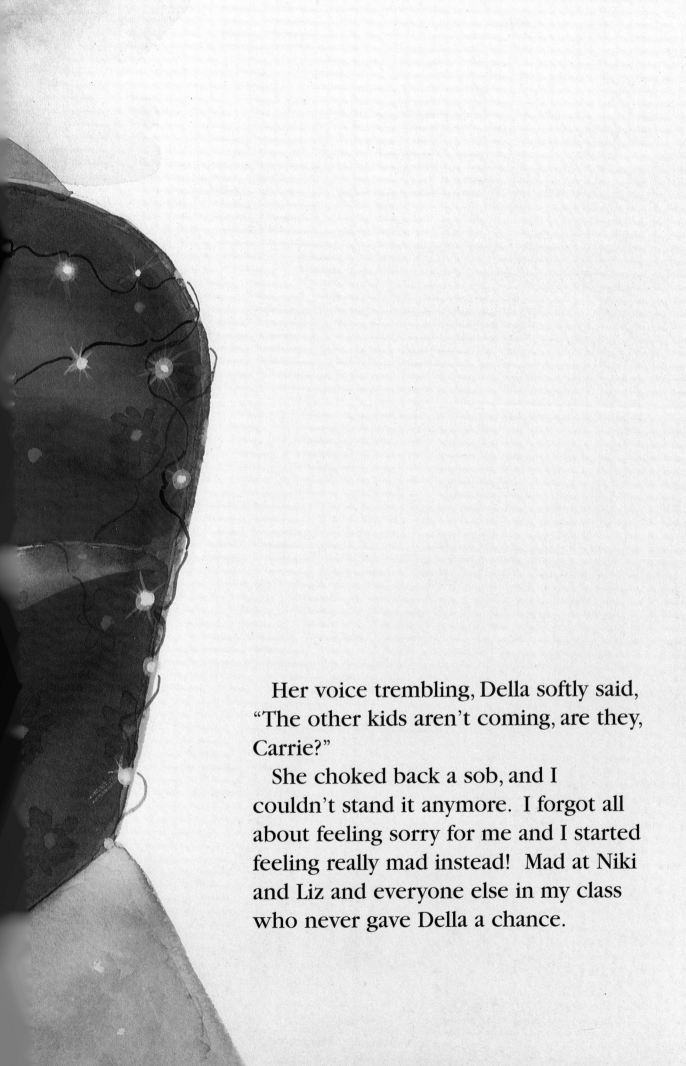

Her voice trembling, Della softly said, "The other kids aren't coming, are they, Carrie?"

She choked back a sob, and I couldn't stand it anymore. I forgot all about feeling sorry for me and I started feeling really mad instead! Mad at Niki and Liz and everyone else in my class who never gave Della a chance.

Before I had time to think about it, I jumped up and yelled out, "WHO NEEDS 'EM?" I took Della's hands in mine and swung her around the room, saying, "What could be better, Della? A huge chocolate cake, just for us, twenty-eight candy cups, just for us, gallons of punch to drink, balloons to toss, and party games to play—all just for us!"

Della looked surprised, then excited. And I was suddenly feeling great!

Della's mother lit the candles on the big cake, and I yelled the Happy Birthday song so loud Della had to laugh and cover her ears. She scrunched her eyes closed and made a wish, and I helped her blow out the tiny flames. The cake was yellow inside with chocolate icing—just like I would have picked—and we each got three roses!

Next, we made party hats with construction paper and glitter glue. Then Della's mom played crazy music and taught us some really cool dances.

Somehow, Della didn't seem that weird anymore. She may not have been exactly like everyone else, but she was so much fun to be with!

When our moms went back into the kitchen to clean up, Della and I talked and talked, and I told her some secrets I had never even told Niki and Liz. Then I remembered her present! "Happy Birthday," I said, "to my new true friend."

Della looked really surprised that I said that. She dropped the balloon she was bouncing and gave me a big hug. I don't think she even cared what was in the box.

She carefully pulled the paper away. "Origami!" she yelled. "I've always wanted to learn this! You barely even knew me and you picked the perfect present for me."

I felt bad then. I remembered how I hadn't wanted to come to the party and how Mom had gone for the present by herself. All I said was, "Well, I know you now."

Mom came out and said it was time for us to go.
"Can Della come over after school on Monday?"
I asked her.
Mom smiled. "I think that's a great idea," she said.

Della came outside with me to say good-bye.

"Thanks . . . ," she whispered, "for everything."

"Don't forget your origami papers on Monday," I reminded her.

Della stood on her front lawn and waved until we turned the corner and I couldn't see her anymore.

Mom squeezed my knee, and I saw she had tears in her eyes. "This could have been a sad, sad birthday for Della," she said, "but because of you, it was a wonderful one. I'm so proud of you."

I knew then why Mom had made me go to the party. Everyone deserves a chance. Della deserved the chance to share her birthday with someone. And I deserved the chance to find a friend like Della.